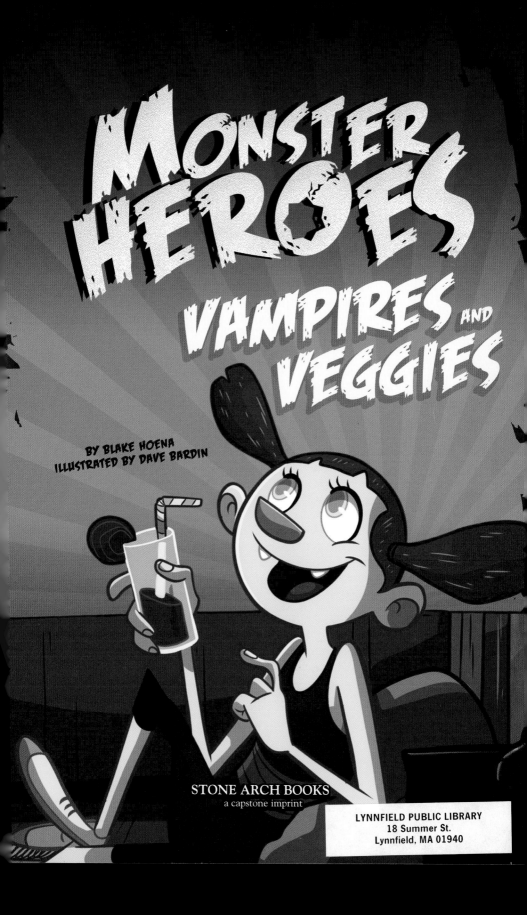

MONSTER HEROES

VAMPIRES AND VEGGIES

BY BLAKE HOENA
ILLUSTRATED BY DAVE BARDIN

STONE ARCH BOOKS
a capstone imprint

Monster Heroes is published by
Stone Arch Books, a Capstone Imprint
1710 Roe Crest Drive
North Mankato, Minnesota 56003
www.mycapstone.com

Library of Congress Cataloging-in-Publication Data
Names: Hoena, B. A., author. | Bardin, Dave (Illustrator), illustrator.
Title: Vampires and veggies / by Blake Hoena ; illustrated by Dave Bardin.
Description: North Mankato, Minnesota : Stone Arch Books, a Capstone imprint,
[2017] | Series: Monster heroes | Summary: Mina is a vampire who prefers
vegetables to blood, so when her parents invite "dinner" guests over, she and her
monster friends come up with a plan to save the unsuspecting guests with pizza.
Identifiers: LCCN 2016006106 | ISBN 9781496537553 (library binding)
Subjects: LCSH: Vampires—Juvenile fiction. | Monsters—Juvenile fiction. |
Heroes—Juvenile fiction. | Friendship—Juvenile fiction. | CYAC: Vampires—
Fiction. | Monsters—Fiction. | Heroes—Fiction. | Friendship—Fiction.
Classification: LCC PZ7.H67127 Vam 2017 | DDC 813.6—dc23
LC record available at http://lccn.loc.gov/2016006106

Book design by: Ted Williams
Photo credit: Krithika Mahalingam Photography (mahalphoto.com), pg 94,
Shutterstock, kasha_malasha, design element

Printed and bound in the United States of America.
009666F16

8/25/17

TABLE OF CONTENTS

MINA *(the Vampire)*

Mina thinks people taste like dirty socks, so beet juice is her snack of choice. Its red color has fooled her parents into thinking that she's a traditional blood-sucking vampire instead of a superhero hopeful. She has the ability to change into a bat or a mouse at will.

Brian is the brainy one amongst his friends. Unlike other zombies, Brian prefers tofu to brains. No matter what sort of trouble is brewing, Brian always comes up with a plan to save the day, like a true superhero.

BRIAN *(the Zombie)*

WILL *(the Ghost)*

Will is quite shy. Luckily he can turn invisible any time he wants because he is a ghost. When Will is doing good deeds, he likes to remain unseen. His invisibility helps him act brave like a real superhero.

With a wave of her wand and a poetic chant, Linda can reverse any magical curse. She hopes to use her magic to help people, just like a superhero would.

LINDA *(the Witch)*

BEET JUICE

Slurp! Mina took a big sip from a glass filled with red liquid.

"Is that . . ." Linda gasped, ". . . blood?"

"Of course not! It's just beet juice," Mina said.

"Ew, that's worse," Linda said. She scrunched up her nose in disgust. "Why do you drink *that*?"

"I drink beet juice so my parents think I drink blood," Mina said. "You know, like a normal vampire."

"Well, it fooled me," Linda said.

"At least it doesn't taste as bad as people do," Mina said.

"Really?" Linda asked. "What do people taste like?"

"Like dirty socks soaked in pickle juice," Mina said.

"Double ew!" Linda said.

Just then, the doorbell rang. Mina and Linda ran to the top of the staircase to see who was at the front door.

It was the new neighbors. Mina's parents greeted two adults.

A boy stood in front of the adults. He was about Mina's age. The boy looked up and waved to the girls.

"We're so glad you could make it," Mina's dad said with an evil grin.

"Yes, we love having people for dinner," Mina's mom said with a matching evil grin.

The girls ran back to Mina's room.

"No, no, no!" Mina said. "This is bad. Really, *really* bad."

"Why? Don't you like having dinner guests?" Linda asked.

"You don't understand," Mina said. "They are not dinner guests. They *are* dinner!"

"Oh!" Linda gulped.

Mina and her friends were not like other monsters. They didn't suck people's blood or hurt people. They helped people because they wanted to be like superheroes.

"We better call Will and Brian," Mina said.

DINNER GUESTS

"Mina!" Mina's mom called. "We need you to come down."

The girls looked at each other, worried. Their friends hadn't arrived yet.

"What should I do?" Mina asked.

Linda shrugged. "I don't know."

"Mina," Mina's dad called. "Come meet Mr. and Mrs. Plasma and their son, Greg."

"I have to go," Mina said.

"When Brian and Will get here," Linda whispered, "we'll think of a plan to save your neighbors. Try to stall."

Mina slowly walked down the stairs. Her parents waited at the bottom. They looked extra excited.

"Hi," the boy said. He seemed very friendly.

"Hey," Mina replied, trying to act normal.

"Mina, please show Greg around," Mina's dad said.

"You should go get a bite to eat in the kitchen," Mina's mom said with a wink.

Mina grabbed Greg's hand. She pulled him into the kitchen.

"Your parents are kind of strange," Greg said. "They keep asking about my blood type and if I take garlic supplements."

Mina sat Greg down at a table. She took a deep breath. She was afraid Greg would think she was a blood-sucking monster too. But she had to warn him about her family.

"We're vampires," Mina whispered.

Then she grinned, to show her him her pointy fangs.

"That's cool!" Greg said.

"You're not afraid?" Mina asked.

"No, not all monsters are scary," Greg said. "My best friend at my old school is a werewolf."

"Yeah, some of us are different," Mina said with a smile.

There was a tap on the kitchen window. It was Will. Mina opened the window to let him in.

"This is my friend Will," Mina said to Greg.

In one hand, Will carried Mina's glass of beet juice.

"Is that blood?" Greg asked.

"No, silly. It's beet juice," Mina said. "I don't drink blood. I'm a vegetarian."

"She drinks beet juice so her parents won't know her secret," Will said.

"Why can't your parents know you don't drink blood?" Greg asked, confused.

"My parents would never understand. They are traditional vampires," Mina said.

"We aren't like other monsters," Will said. "We like to help people."

"Like superheroes?" Greg asked.

"Exactly. We need everyone to think we are scary monsters," Mina said. "Then we can secretly help people."

"Enough talking," Will said. He held up a red marker.

"What's that for?" Greg asked.

"It's part of our plan to save you and your parents," Will said. "And to keep Mina's secret a secret."

Will floated over to Greg. With the marker, he drew two red dots on Greg's neck.

"Perfect!" Will said. "Now I'd better go before Mina's parents see me."

"Thanks, Will!" Mina said.

"Happy to help," Will said as he floated out the window and disappeared.

PIZZA PLEASE

Just then Mina's parents entered the kitchen. They looked at the red marks on Greg's neck. They saw Mina sipping her beet juice and smiled.

"I hope you are enjoying your snack," Mina's mom said.

"Now it's time for our dinner," Mina's dad said.

Before they could start dinner, the doorbell rang. Mina and Greg poked their heads out of the kitchen to watch.

Will and Linda watched from the top of the stairs, hoping their plan would work.

When the door opened, their friend Brian stepped inside.

"Pizza delivery!" he shouted.

Mina's parents looked confused.

"I guess we're having pizza for dinner," Mina's dad said.

"Your plan worked!" Mina said.

"Of course it did," Brian said.

"And we made a new friend," Linda said.

Will and Greg could only nod
and mumble. They were too busy
stuffing their faces with pizza.

BLAKE A. HOENA

Blake A. Hoena grew up in central Wisconsin, where he wrote stories about robots conquering the moon and trolls lumbering around the woods behind his parents house. He now lives in Minnesota and continues to write about fun things like space aliens and superheroes. Blake has written more than fifty chapter books and graphic novels for children.

DAVE BARDIN

Dave Bardin studied illustration at Cal State Fullerton while working as an art teacher. As an artist, Dave has worked on many different projects for television, books, comics, and animation. In his spare time Dave enjoys watching documentaries, listening to podcasts, traveling, and spending time with friends and family. He works out of Los Angeles, CA.

VAMPIRE GLOSSARY

beet—a plant with a root that can be eaten; a beet root is dark red in color

blood—a red liquid found in people that *most* vampires drink as food

blood type—one of the four main types of blood: A, B, AB, O; people have different blood types depending on certain substances found in their blood; O is the most common and AB the rarest, and also the type vampires like the most.

garlic—a strong-smelling plant used for cooking; vampires don't like garlic or like sucking the blood from people who eat a lot of garlic.

supplement—a substance added to something to make it complete, like garlic added to a vitamin pill

vegetarian—a person who doesn't eat meat, or a vampire who doesn't drink blood

werewolf—a person who turns into a wolf-like monster during a full moon

THINK ABOUT IT

1. Mina drinks beet juice instead of blood. Why is knowing this important to the story?

2. Mina was scared to tell Greg she was a vampire. Were you surprised by Greg's reaction? Why or why not?

3. Do you think Mina should tell her parents that she doesn't drink blood? Explain your answer.

WRITE ABOUT IT

1. How do you think Mina's parents felt when the pizza arrived? Write a paragraph describing their feelings.

2. Pretend you are Greg and write a journal entry about your night at Mina's house.

3. The monsters used a pizza plan to solve their big problem. Write up your own plan to save Greg and his parents.

THE FUN DOESN'T STOP HERE!

Discover more at www.capstonekids.com